From the west
Clouds come hurrying with the wind
Turning sharply
Here and there
Like a plague of locusts
Whirling,
Tossing up things on its tail
Like a madman chasing nothing…"
— **David Rubadiri**

Author- Fortune Omosola

ISBN (Paperback)- 978-1-917267-50-2

ISBN (E-Book)-978-1-917267-51-9

Year Published- 2025

Published by Nubian Republic Ltd Uk on behalf of Raffia Press Nigeria Limited an imprint of Palmwine Publishing Limited Nigeria

Email: info@palmwinepublishing.com

Address-Nigeria: 1A Jos Road Bukuru, Plateau State, Nigeria.

www.palmwinepublishing.com

www.raffiapress.com

www.nuciferaanalysis.com

Table of Contents

Table of Contents

Chapter One: The Tree by the Gutter

I make bad decisions until it becomes a tree ripe for harvest.

My name is Kola, and I was born on a Monday evening, just before the rains came. My mother told me that the first sound I ever made was not a cry, but a cough, a dry, brittle thing, like the clatter of broomsticks on bare cement. The midwife, Mama Eunice, took one look at me, wrapped in tattered Ankara cloth, and said I had the face of a child who had lived before. In Malete, they say that children like that often return to settle a score with the world.

We lived in a one-room face-me-I-face-you with a zinc roof that rattled each time the harmattan wind passed like a god in a hurry. Our compound was a collection of souls waging war against the economy: mama with her overworked spine and endless trays of fried akara; Baba Shedrack, the drunk carpenter who spoke only to lizards; and children who learned arithmetic from the price of sachet water. Behind our house was a gutter so wide it could swallow a goat, and next to it, an orange tree, bent, bruised, but always flowering. That tree was my hiding place, my cathedral, my internet café, and sometimes, my pulpit.

My mother called me her miracle. She said I came from her womb after five miscarriages, and every time I stared into her tired eyes—eyes that held both holy fire and unspoken suffering, I knew that I owed her something big, something god-sized. She sold everything from mangoes to second-hand bras, just to keep me in school. She had faith like fire, the kind that melted even logic. But I, I had my eyes on wires, screens, and the cold gospel of technology.

While my mates played football with bare feet and angry knees, I sat cross-legged beside the orange tree with broken radios and dismantled flash drives. I could turn scrap into sound, solder wires like prayer beads, and type faster than our class typist. I wasn't just a nerd; I was an escape artist, hacking my way through poverty one megabyte at a time.

But Malete had a way of reminding you that dreams are delicate things. Sometimes, it came as a NEPA outage that swallowed your unsaved project. Other times, it came as a gang of street boys who demanded *"tithe"* for walking past their turf. Once, it came as hunger, the kind that made your stomach sound like a talking drum.

Evenings were the hardest. My mother would kneel on her raffia mat, praying in tongues that sounded like war songs, while I tried to debug lines of code on a half-lit screen. There were nights she called me her pastor, other nights she called me a prodigal. I called myself nothing, I just wanted out.

The older I grew, the more I understood the rituals of our survival. There was a way to greet the landlord if you hadn't paid rent, firm voice, eyes low, fingers crossed behind your back. There was a way to avoid fights in the queue for fetching water, say *"abeg"* twice and call them "uncle" even if they're younger than you. And there was a way to lie to yourself that tomorrow would be better, say it quickly, before sleep steals your hope.

I remember the day I first saw a laptop, not in school, not in church, but in the hands of a corper from Abuja who came to do IT training at our community center. He wore perfume that smelled like promises and shoes that didn't make noise. When he opened the screen and typed "print ('Hello, World')", I knew I had just witnessed magic. That night, I told my mother I wanted to study computer science. She paused mid-prayer, looked at me like I had announced I wanted to marry a ghost, and said, "Kọ́lá, your head too dey hot...abeggi!"

Still, I persisted. I started fixing phones in secret, downloading coding tutorials using borrowed MTN data, and saving every naira from mending electric fans and laptop chargers. I worked like a man running from something he couldn't name. Perhaps I was trying to outrun the ghost of my father, who left when I was two and only returned in whispers.

But no matter how fast I ran, Malete held on.

The streets knew my name, but not my dreams. My friends knew my jokes, but not my fears. And my mother—ah, my mother—she knew everything, yet never asked too many questions. She only said, "A boy who carries a torch must be ready to burn."

I didn't know then that the same light that guided me would also set me ablaze.

Chapter Two: God of Small Hustles

In Malete, everybody hustled. Even God.

He hustled for attention between beer parlour arguments and loudspeakers from white garment churches. He hustled for space between okada crashes and midnight shouts of "thief, thief!" God was busy, and often absent. So we created gods of our own, small, efficient gods who didn't need praise worship before they blessed you. Data bundles. Malams who doubled money. Senior boys who knew "one guy in Abuja."

By my second year at Unillorin, I had learned to serve all of them.

The hostel where I stayed was called "Heavenly Glory Villa," but it had neither glory nor heaven. Just peeling paint, leaking bathrooms, and rooms packed with dreams sweating in the heat. Every morning began with a familiar chant: "Make una bring light na! kai!!" And every evening, the same chorus of sighs when NEPA didn't answer. My roommates were all broken prophets in their own way, two were Yahoo boys, one was an ex-seminarian turned forex trader, and one just slept all day, blaming depression for his poor CGPA.

I kept to myself mostly. I spent my mornings in lectures I barely listened to, and my nights in café lounges where the real education happened. It was there I learned how to unlock phones without passwords, bypass school Wi-Fi firewalls, and install cracked software from Russian forums. People started calling me "Kola the Fixer." I liked it. It felt like power, even if temporary.

But fixing phones couldn't pay for everything. Especially not the hospital bills piling in a brown envelope back home.

My mother had started coughing again. Not the dry kind. Wet, phlegmy. The kind that ends in a whisper. She never told me directly. She only said things like, "God is testing me again," or "Kọlá, don't worry about me. Just do well in school." But I knew what that meant. So I did what every desperate son of Malete does when God delays, I found my own hustle.

It started with SIM swaps. A guy from Abuja named Smallz showed me how. He would buy customer details from corrupt telco staff, clone the SIM, and drain whatever mobile bank accounts were linked to it. I wasn't proud of it, but I only wrote the scripts that automated the process. I told myself I wasn't a thief. I was just... helping code the theft.

One afternoon, while sitting in the back of the school library pretending to study, I got a call from Smallz.

"Guy, I swear down, you be genius," he said, his voice heavy with excitement. "That your script work like jazz. I don withdraw 850k just now. E be like film."

I didn't laugh. Something in my stomach turned. Eight hundred and fifty thousand naira. More than my mother had seen in ten years. I imagined what she would say if she knew her son—the one she once called "prophet", was now indirectly robbing pensioners through airtime top-ups.

But the money kept coming.

And God? God kept quiet.

That was when I met Halima.

She came like harmattan—soft, sudden, and impossible to ignore. A final-year Mass Communication student with eyes like she'd seen too much for her age. She was dressed in a deep blue hijab the first day I saw her, standing outside the library, holding a battered copy of Things Fall Apart. The irony was too loud.

She approached me after a departmental seminar and said, "You asked a question about data surveillance and privacy. I liked the way you phrased it... like you weren't just trying to sound smart."

I didn't know what to say. Nobody had ever complimented my brain outside of code.

We started talking. First about school, then about faith. I told her I wasn't really sure about God anymore. That I believed in things I could debug. She smiled and said, "Even prophets doubt. It's not doubt that makes you fall—it's silence."

She was unlike any girl I'd met, smart, blunt, funny. And dangerous.

Because the more I liked her, the more I lied to her.

I never told her about the SIM jobs. Or the drinking. Or the night I almost got arrested by DSS agents in Ilorin for helping a guy unlock a "politician's stolen iPad." I told her only about the dreams—the company I wanted to build one day, the life I was coding for myself. She liked those versions. So I kept giving them to her.

But real life has a way of catching up to you.

It happened during Ramadan. Halima had invited me to her family house in Ilorin for Iftar. Her father was a retired civil servant with kind eyes and a voice like a muezzin. Her mother served eba and egusi with smoked fish that tasted like forgiveness. That evening felt like a warm bath I didn't want to leave.

When I got back to my hostel, there were two missed calls from Smallz and one text that simply read:

"Guy, lay low. One of our boys don cast."

My heart froze.

I turned off my phone, shut my laptop, and stared at the wall for a long time. In that moment, the orange tree from Malete returned to my mind. I imagined it now without fruit—bare, grey, haunted.

Days passed. Then weeks.

Campus felt colder. Halima sensed something. She asked if I was okay. I told her I was just tired.

But the truth was louder in my ears.

I was tired of fear.

Tired of pretending.

Tired of being hunted by my own ambition.

One night, while walking back from night class, I passed the University mosque. The call to prayer rose in the wind like a song from the ancestors. I stopped and listened.

And for the first time in years, I whispered something that might've been a prayer:

"Olorun… if you're still awake, show me how to stop being the devil I've become."

....

I didn't go back to coding for three weeks. I deleted every script that could tie me to Smallz, threw away the SIM cards, and even changed hostels. My new place was a bit closer to Oke-Odo market, smaller, lonelier, and with a neighbour who listened to Fuji from dawn till dusk.

One hot Friday, I was walking past a suya stand near the park when Halima called. "Oga Fixer," she said, teasing. "You don change hostel and you no tell your best customer."

I managed a weak laugh. "I dey try lay low, jare. That my old place dey too hot."

"For laptop or for conscience?" she asked, then paused. "Sorry. That was a bit sharp. I just… I haven't seen you in weeks. You okay?"

I wanted to lie. Say I was fine. Say I was just working hard. But something in her voice stopped me.

"Halima," I said, voice lower now. "You ever feel like you're becoming someone you were once afraid of?"

There was a brief silence on the line. The kind that wasn't empty, but full of unspoken things.

"All the time," she replied. "Especially when I pray less."

We met that Sunday. I took her to a roadside buka—not romantic, not fancy, but it had the best amala in all of Kwara. She wore a simple black gown and a scarf that caught the sunlight in soft waves. We sat under a rickety umbrella while flies tried to join us.

I watched her eat. Not in that creepy way some guys do, but with a strange ache in my chest. This girl, so grounded, so unbothered, was sitting across from a boy who had once helped drain an old man's pension. If she knew, would she still smile at me?

"I feel like you're hiding," she said, dropping her spoon.

I didn't respond. "Not from me, necessarily," she added, "but from something. Or someone."

"Maybe," I said. She leaned forward. "You ever hear the story of Sango's third son?"

I shook my head.

She smiled. "It's not in any real mythology. My grandfather used to tell it when he wanted to warn us about secrets. Sango had a third son nobody talked about. He was brilliant, brave, but also dangerous. He stole fire from his father's shrine and hid it in a clay pot. Thought he could tame it. One day, the pot broke, and the fire consumed everything, his house, his mother, even himself."

She paused, letting the words burn their way into me. "You know what my grandfather used to say after that?"

"What?"

"'The fire that warms you can also eat your bones, if you sleep too close.'"

I stared at my plate. My appetite had gone.

"Halima..." I started. "I've done some things. Nothing crazy. But... things."

She didn't blink. "I'm not who I told you I was," I said.

She nodded slowly. "None of us are. But if you're going to walk through fire, Kola, at least wear your own shoes. Not borrowed ones."

We left the buka in silence.

As we walked past a vendor selling second-hand laptops, I felt something cold trickle down my spine. A police van was parked across the road. Two officers stood by, scanning faces. My stomach flipped. One of them—the taller one—looked like the DSS agent I'd seen during the botched iPad gig. Or maybe my mind was playing tricks.

Halima noticed my shift. "You okay?"

"Y-yeah," I stammered. "Just remembered I have a test tomorrow."

"You sure?" "Positive." I replied.

She nodded, but her eyes stayed on me longer than they should.

....

Back at the hostel, I shut the curtain, turned off my phone, and sat on the floor for hours. The fan squeaked above me like a warning. I could feel something coming. A reckoning. Not from the police. Not even from Smallz.

From myself.

That night, Halima sent a message. One line. No emojis. No extra full stops.

"Let me know when you're ready to stop hiding." I didn't reply.

Because I didn't know how.

Chapter Three: Between Altars

I had barely slept when the knock came. Not a polite one.

Not the kind that neighbours used to borrow matches or curse you for playing music too loud. This was a knock that came with weight. Urgency. Like something on the other side wanted permission to drag you out of the world you'd built for yourself.

I froze. My heart began thumping like the drumbeats before Egungun comes out in June.

Another knock. Firmer.

Then a voice.

"Open this door now. We no get time!"

Two men. One Yoruba, the other with an accent I couldn't place.

DSS? Police? Area boys?

I scanned my one-room cell. Laptop: off. Burner phones: gone. Scripts: deleted. Only my school bag, a pile of used notebooks, and a plastic bucket of soaking clothes remained.

I tiptoed to the door and whispered, "Who be that?"

A pause.

Then, "You dey ask who be that? We no be landlord. Open before we break this door."

I cracked the door open an inch. They pushed it wide.

Two men in mufti stepped in. The first wore a navy-blue kaftan and cheap leather sandals. His face was thin, lined with irritation. The other had a camouflage cap pulled low. Something in his eyes—hard, unmoved—told me they weren't just here to chat.

"You be Kola, abi?" the man in kaftan asked.

"Yes, sir," I said, already sweating.

"You get small minute? We wan ask you something for junction."

"For what?" I asked.

He smiled. The kind of smile that didn't touch his eyes.

"Na just normal questioning. You fit follow us peacefully or…"

The second man adjusted his shirt slightly—just enough for me to catch a glimpse of the black handle tucked at his waist.

I nodded. "Let me wear my slippers."

They let me step outside with them. As we walked past the corner shop, Mama Chinyere gave me a long, suspicious look. She was a gossip. By nightfall, half of Oke-Odo would be whispering that "that tech boy don chop gbege."

We turned into an alley behind the hostel, empty except for a hawker frying bean cakes over a smoking drum.

Suddenly, the first man stopped. He looked at me squarely.

"You dey work with one guy, Smallz?"

My chest tightened. "No," I lied. "I no sabi any Smallz."

He sighed, long and tired. "We go try again. You dey work with one guy wey dey unlock phones, carry money from people account, use BVN wire money go outside?"

"Sir, I be student. I no sabi all those things."

The second man reached into his pocket and brought out a phone. He opened the gallery and showed me a screenshot.

It was from WhatsApp.

My number.

My exact number.

Chatting with Smallz.

My message: "Code go run sharp. Just make sure your VPN dey solid."

I went numb. "I fit explain..." I mumbled.

The man in kaftan raised a hand. "Kola, relax. We no wan arrest you... for now. Na why we come like this. Gentle."

"Then what do you want?" I was anxious and filled with trepidation.

He looked at me. His voice dropped low.

"Your guy don cast. Dem pick Smallz for Wuse last week. Him mention your name."

Silence.

I felt like the ground under me had started cracking.

"But…" I began, "I no… I didn't steal. I just wrote the tools."

The man in camouflage scoffed. "You think say na difference? If person use your knife kill goat, you no go follow chop curse?"

I looked away.

Kaftan-man leaned closer. "Look, we no wan disgrace you. We no even need to take you station, yet. Just bring everything wey fit link you to the job. Laptop. External drive. Flash. Anything. No do pass yourself."

"Okay, sir. Tomorrow," I said quickly. "I fit gather everything tonight."

He nodded. "Tomorrow morning. Nine sharp. Don't run. If you run, you go make am worse."

As they left, I stood in the alley like something forgotten.

My legs were jelly. My palms, wet.

Smallz. That bastard. That Judas.

He sang.

That night, I couldn't breathe.

I powered on my laptop again, not to code, but to wipe. I deleted every log, encrypted my hard drive, formatted the external drive, and for good measure, burned two old SIM cards on a charcoal stove behind the hostel.

By 2 a.m., the smell of melted plastic was all that was left of the life I had built in secret.

And then, like fate itself remembered I hadn't suffered enough. Halima called.

I didn't want to answer. But I did.

"Hey," I said, forcing calm.

"You okay?" she asked. "You sound far."

"I'm fine. Just tired."

A pause.

"Someone from school texted me. Said some guys came looking for you today. That true?"

I sighed. "Yeah. But it's not as bad as it sounds."

"Kola…"

"I'm handling it."

She was quiet again. "You're spiraling."

"I'm fine." I adjusted, sternly looking through what I was doing.

"No, you're drowning. And you're pretending the water isn't in your mouth already."

I felt something break. A small crack.

"Then help me," I said.

"I can't help someone who won't tell me what he's fighting."

"I'm fighting regret," I snapped. "And hunger. And fear. And the stupid version of me who thought God was just a software glitch."

The line went silent.

Then her voice returned, soft, almost a whisper.

"I'm still here, Kola. But don't wait too long. Fire doesn't wait."

The call ended. I stared at the screen for a long time then I opened a blank document and started typing.

Chapter Four: Ashes for Skin

I didn't go to the police station.

Instead, I went to church.

Not because I was seeking salvation but because I needed to hide somewhere God wouldn't expect to find me.

It was a Wednesday morning. Light rain dragged itself lazily across the Ilorin sky. I hadn't slept, hadn't bathed, hadn't changed the clothes from the day before. My laptop was zipped inside a black backpack. I wore a hoodie, face low, pace slow.

The church was an old Catholic building in Sabo-Oke, behind the abattoir. The kind of church where pigeons outnumber parishioners, and paint peels like God gave up halfway. A security man, lean and weathered, stared at me as I walked in. I told him I was there for "special prayers." He didn't ask further. Everyone had secrets in that area. Mine wasn't special.

I sat in the fourth pew, beside a woman praying in Yoruba so urgently, you'd think she was owed a refund. I bowed my head, but I didn't pray. I just stared at the wooden crucifix above the altar and wondered how someone nailed to wood could still feel more free than me.

After an hour, I slipped out through the side entrance.

The city smelled like wet sand and roadside akara. I headed for a small printing café near Gaa-Akanbi, where nobody knew me. There, I printed my fake NYSC call-up letter, a backup plan if things got worse. Not that I wanted to go to camp. But people trusted you more in Nigeria if you were wearing khaki and shouting "one love."

It was there I got the call.

The screen read: Uncle Tunji, Home.

I hadn't saved the number, but I knew it by heart. The voice on the other end was shaking.

"Kọ́lá… your mother don collapse."

My legs gave way before my mind did. I dropped onto the pavement in front of the café, people brushing past me like I was part of the furniture.

"She dey hospital?" I asked.

"No," he said. "She no make am."

Just like that.

No last words.

No warning.

No miracle.

I didn't cry. Not then. Not even when I got on a night bus back to Malete with nothing but my backpack and a dying phone. The road from Ilorin to Malete had always been bad, filled with potholes the size of destiny but that night, it felt like a journey to the land of forgotten gods.

My mother had been buried before I arrived.

Uncle Tunji met me at the entrance of the compound with puffy eyes and a half-empty bottle of Seaman's Aromatic Schnapps.

"She say make we no put am fridge. Make we bury her same day."

"Why?"

"She say cold never help anybody survive this world."

I nodded. I couldn't feel my hands.

The compound looked smaller. The orange tree had shed its leaves. There was a new crack in the wall near the entrance. The woman selling pap out front said, "Kola, pele o," and I almost punched the wind out of her.

I didn't enter our room. I sat beside the gutter. The same one I used to play beside. I sat there till dawn, until the muezzin called for morning prayers and dogs started barking at things they couldn't see.

Grief does not always wear black. Sometimes it comes in the sound of a woman sweeping before sunrise. Sometimes, it smells like petrol from a generator that shouldn't be on that early.

At 7:12 a.m., I opened my backpack and looked at the laptop.

There, in the Recycle Bin, was my confession file. I hadn't deleted it. Just renamed it again.

Now it read: *Version2_NoGod.docx*

....

By 9 a.m., I was back on the road.

Not to Ilorin. Not to school. Not to church.

I took a bus to Abuja.

The interview I'd been preparing for the tech internship that was supposed to change my life was two days away. I hadn't confirmed attendance. I hadn't even rehearsed. But I needed something that didn't remind me of my mother's coughing or her empty bed.

On the bus were 16 of us. A mix of traders, students, corps members, and a woman with three restless children who kept throwing puff-puff at each other.

I sat by the window and stared outside, counting billboards that advertised dreams: "APPLY FOR CANADA PR!", "NAIRA INVESTMENT THAT PAYS IN DOLLARS!", "BECOME A TECH BRO IN 3 MONTHS!"

It was somewhere near Moro that the road turned strange.

First came the makeshift checkpoint—two logs across the road, manned by four men in plain clothes with scarves around their faces. The bus slowed.

"Is this SARS?" someone asked nervously.

"No be SARS," said the driver. "Dem no dey wear slippers."

He wasn't wrong.

As we approached, one of the men raised a shotgun. The driver stopped.

They began dragging people out.

The woman screamed. One of the corps members protested and got slapped so hard his beret flew into the bush.

I held my breath.

When it was my turn, they searched my bag.

"What be this?" one asked, holding up the laptop.

"Na school laptop," I lied.

The leader, a dark man with a tribal mark that curved like lightning, said, "Put am back. Carry am."

They herded us into the bush, guns behind our backs like angry shadows. Fifteen minutes in, someone tried to run.

They shot him. No warning.

I heard the thud. Then the gurgle. Then silence. That was when I knew we weren't getting ransomed.

This wasn't kidnapping.

This was elimination.

But fate, that wicked playwright, had other plans.

As they pushed us to kneel by a gully edge, an argument broke out among them.

The youngest of the men—barely older than me—kept saying, "We no suppose kill everybody. We suppose collect the phones, collect money. Wetin be this now?!"

The leader shouted him down.That's when it happened.

The boy snapped.

He raised his gun and fired at the leader. A wild, panicked shot. Missed the head, but hit the neck.

Blood was everywhere. Then chaos.

Another gunman fired back at the boy. Another shot one of the hostages by mistake.

I didn't think. I rolled sideways, grabbed the fallen leader's AK-47, and fired—three wild shots that kicked back like thunder.

I didn't aim. I just ran.

Behind me, screams. Bullets. Another explosion of sound. But I ran like something chased me that wasn't of this world.

Through the bush. Through pain. Through breath that burned.

By the time I emerged near a sleepy hamlet on the edge of Moro, I was bleeding from my arm. My shirt was torn. My hand shook as I dropped the weapon into a muddy trench.

Then I heard shouting. Locals had seen me.

Someone yelled, "He get gun!"

Another: "Na one of them o!"

I tried to explain. I lifted my hands.

But it was too late.

The hunters had become the hunted.

My eyes blurred a bit as I staggered backwards, completely clueless of what had happened. My thought process was stone cold blocked.

Chapter Five: The Boy With the Bloodied Hands

They say the gods don't speak anymore.

But in Moro, that sleepy village on the edge of the forgotten, the gods had just screamed.

The sound of gunfire had been carried by the wind, like a hymn of death. By the time the villagers reached the scene, the air smelled of smoke, fear, and wet leaves. A goat bleated somewhere in the distance, as if echoing the cries of the survivors.

Kola ran.

His legs ached, his arm throbbed from the cut where a thorny branch had kissed him too deep. His shirt was soaked in sweat and blood—not all of it his. Behind him, voices. Chasing. Angry. Alarmed.

"He get gun!"

"One of dem!"

He tried to shout, to explain. "I'm not one of them! They kidnapped me! I escaped!"

But in Nigeria, innocence is not a language most people understand.

A man emerged from the side with a cutlass. Kola ducked, rolled into a yam mound, and scrambled up again.

He burst into a compound, startling a woman pounding yam with rhythmic fury.

"Jesu! Who you be?"

"Please! I need help! I was kidnapped—"

Before he could finish, two boys entered through the back gate, one wielding a hoe. Kola turned, jumped over a chicken coop, and vanished into the bush again.

By nightfall, Kola found himself hiding under a disused water tank behind a missionary clinic. His phone had died. His strength was gone. His stomach churned with hunger and dread.

And then came the dream.

His mother, wearing her old Ankara wrapper, walking barefoot on the red soil.

"Kola, my pikin, you go run forever? You think you fit hide from spirits that dance during the day?"

He tried to hold her hand, but she vanished into smoke.

When Kola woke, it was to the sensation of cold steel against his cheek.

A gun.

"If you move, I go scatter your head here," the voice said. Female. Gritty. Familiar.

His eyes adjusted to the dim light. Standing above him was a young woman in a black hijab, holding a rusted rifle with one hand. Her face bore a long scar that started at her right brow and curved down like a crescent moon.

"Halima?" he croaked.

She frowned. "You sabi my name?"

"You used to hawk groundnut near campus gate. You lived in Malete. I gave you my old phone once."

Her grip on the gun loosened slightly. She looked him over.

"You be Kola? Kola wey dem say na tech wizard?"

He nodded.

"Why you dey here like rat wey dem soak?"

He told her. Everything. From the bus ride, to the chaos, to the gun, to the mistaken identity.

She listened. Arms crossed. Face unreadable.

When he finished, she exhaled sharply.

"Omo, your own bad reach. But if na true, you no suppose stay here. Moro people don dey para. Dem swear say anybody wey come bush this week na bandit. Even vigilante don mobilize."

Kola winced. "I need to get out. I need to report this. But I can't just walk into a station. They'll think I'm guilty."

She looked around. Then she knelt beside him. "My elder brother na hunter. Dem dey trust am. Maybe he fit help sneak you out. But you gats lie low for now. I go bring you food. Don't move."

Kola touched her arm. "Thank you."

She stood. "Na so. But no go think say na film you dey act. Moro no dey joke. If dem catch you, dem go use you do example."

The next two days blurred.

Halima returned at dusk and dawn with bread, mangoes, and water from the borehole.

Kola hid, prayed, rewrote his story in his head a thousand times. He imagined walking into the police station. He imagined them listening, nodding, believing. He imagined clearing his name.

But reality in Nigeria rarely matches the imagination.

On the third night, Halima arrived with news.

"Dem don find one of the kidnappers body near Okuta river. Dem say he be Fulani. Dem dey plan rally."

"A rally?"

"To protest government failure. But you know how e dey be. E fit turn riot. Moro people no dey smile again."

Kola wiped his face. "We have to move. Tonight."

She hesitated. "I go talk to my brother. But if anything happen..." she didn't finish.

By midnight, they crept through the bush paths.

Halima led. Her brother, Kabiru, a tall man with fierce eyes and a dane gun, brought up the rear. Kola stayed in the middle, limping slightly.

They passed a banana plantation, a dried stream, and an abandoned petrol station where crickets sang like choirs.

At the edge of town, near the main road, they heard it.

A voice.

"Stop there! Who goes?"

Flashlight beams sliced through the dark. Four men. Armed. Vigilantes.

Kabiru raised a hand. "Na me, Kabiru. I dey patrol."

One of the men stepped forward. "Who be this boy?"

"Na my cousin from Ilorin. Him enter problem for road, I bring am come house."

The man narrowed his eyes. "Which part Ilorin?"

Kola opened his mouth. Brain blank.

"Taiwo road," Halima answered smoothly. "We go bury him mama last week."

The man grunted. Looked Kola over. Then stepped aside.

"Make una waka well. Moro no safe again."

Kola exhaled only when they were far enough.

"You're good at lying," he said to Halima.

She smiled, bitterly. "When you dey survive, lie dey learn your name."

At dawn, Kabiru dropped him by the junction to Jebba.

A bus idled there, half full. Destination: Abuja. Kola turned to Halima. "I don't have money."

She pressed a folded note into his hand. "Na small change. Use am reach city. From there, your leg fit find your destiny."

Kola felt something hard rise in his throat. "I won't forget this. Ever."

She nodded. "Na promise."

As the bus pulled away, he watched her shrink into the dust.

Inside the bus, silence reigned. People dozed. A baby cried softly. Kola stared out at the passing bush.

He had escaped death.

He had watched men die.

He had buried his mother in absentia.

He had held a gun.

But something inside had cracked open.

He wasn't just running from Moro anymore.

He was running from himself.

Chapter Six: Halima's Shadow

The nights in Moro were never completely dark. Even with the power out and the moon hiding, there was always a flicker of light—the shimmer of bush lanterns, or the way stars watched silently over sins and secrets. Kola sat behind the water tank, hands locked between his knees, eyes darting with every rustle in the grass.

Halima had brought him food again—boiled yam and palm oil this time. She didn't say much, just dropped the bag beside him, adjusted her scarf, and turned like the wind, disappearing into the shadows.

But tonight was different. She came back.

He didn't hear her approach. One moment he was staring at a moth fluttering near the tank, the next, she was there, crouching beside him.

"Dem dey plan something," she whispered.

Kola's heart skipped. "Who?"

"The vigilante boys. Say dem go sweep the whole stretch of bush from the primary school fence reach the yam fields. Dem swear say the person wey escape from that kidnapping incident dey hide here."

Kola's lips turned dry. He touched the rifle, still wrapped in torn cloth, buried beneath a broken bucket. "What should I do?"

Halima looked at him, really looked. Her eyes, big and brown, held stories of their own.

"You fit run again?"

"I don't know where to go. Even if I do, I look like one of them. This gun, these clothes..."

She exhaled slowly. Then sat beside him.

"I sabi one road. E dey inside bush. My papa use am during Biafra war, dem say. E lead reach an abandoned cocoa station wey still get path to Ogbomosho express. If you waka well, you fit reach the road. Maybe someone fit help you."

Kola hesitated. "And you?"

She gave a bitter laugh. "Me? Moro know me. Nobody go question me. But you? Your skin dey shout wahala."

He chuckled weakly. "You talk like say I be juju."

"Wetin you be no concern me," she said, rising. "But you gats move before sunrise. Dem go start the sweep around seven. I go come back around four. Dress light. Hide the gun inside yam sack. I go find you torchlight and knife."

He stood too, touching her elbow. "Halima... thank you."

She looked away. "No thank me yet. Moro get eyes. And sometimes, the ground dey talk. Just pray say your feet no land for where spirits dey bath."

At 3:57 AM, she returned.

A torchlight. Two sachets of water. A knife with a broken handle. And a faded green wrapper.

"Tie am like say you be farmer. Carry the sack for shoulder. No look anybody for face. If dem stop you, say you dey go farm for your aunty wey get cocoa field. Her name na Mama Bola. Dem sabi am."

Kola nodded.

They walked in silence, past the back of the dispensary, into a narrow trail swallowed by cassava leaves and pawpaw trees. The air smelled of dawn and damp earth. A goat bleated in the distance. A rooster crowed once, then stopped, like it had second thoughts.

When they reached the fork in the trail, she stopped.

"From here, na you and your destiny. You go reach a red gate with rust. Beside am na broken signboard. Follow the path wey bend left. Don't look back."

Kola turned. Their eyes met.

He wanted to say something poetic, something noble, but all that came out was, "If I make it out, I'll come back for you."

Halima smirked. "Oga escapee, make you just go first. I no dey do love story for bush."

They laughed quietly. And then he was gone.

He walked fast. Quietly. Every shadow looked like a soldier. Every stick felt like a gun's barrel. But he kept going. Past the rusted gate. Past the termite-infested signboard that read: **Welcome to Igbo-Ade Cocoa Farm Cooperative.**

The forest opened up slightly. The stars dimmed.

Then he heard it. Voices. Male. Close.

"You sure say na this way e pass?"

"Dem say dem see wrapper for bush. E still fresh."

He crouched instantly, heart hammering. He moved behind a mound of cocoa husks and lay flat, the sack covering him.

Footsteps approached.

A torchlight flickered. "You see am?"

"Na yam sack be this. Empty."

Kola didn't breathe.

"Nothing dey here. Make we check the ridge. Maybe na animal dem see."

They moved on.

When the bush quieted, he rose and ran. Ran till his legs screamed. Till his chest heaved. Till his head rang.

Then he tripped. Fell into a gully.

His face hit something cold. Hard. Metal.

A corpse.

A man, wrapped in a vigilante vest, throat slit, eyes open, staring straight at him.

Kola scrambled back. His scream died in his throat.

Footsteps again.

"You hear that?"

Another torchlight.

Kola grabbed the vigilante's gun. Without thinking, he fired once into the air.

The bush exploded with chaos. Birds. Voices. Running feet.

He didn't wait. He fled, cutting through the cocoa trees like a madman, blood on his hands, fire in his legs.

He broke through the last wall of trees and found himself on a narrow tarred road.

A trailer rumbled past.

Kola raised his hands, waving like a man possessed. The trailer didn't stop.

But a small Peugeot 504, driven by a priest, did.

Father Mbakwe.

"Jesus wept! My son, you look like you escaped Hell."

Kola collapsed into the backseat, whispering, "Maybe I did. Maybe I'm still inside it."

The priest sped off. In his rearview mirror, the bushes danced with shadows.

Behind them, Moro slept again—but not peacefully.

Chapter Seven: The Priest's Burden

The Peugeot 504 hissed and grumbled as it made its way down the cracked tar road. The sun had not yet risen, but a pale orange streak was beginning to unfurl in the east like an ancestral cloth, heavy with prophecy. Kola sat hunched in the back seat, arms wrapped around himself, as if his body were trying to keep his spirit from spilling out. His clothes reeked of sweat and soil, and the wrapper Halima had given him was now torn at the seam, flapping loosely like a dying banner.

Father Mbakwe glanced at him through the rearview mirror, brow creased with worry. "You haven't said a word since we left that place," he said gently. "And your eyes, my son... they look like they've seen spirits."

Kola looked up, lips trembling. "I've seen worse."

The priest turned his eyes back to the road. "Do you want to tell me what happened?"

Kola hesitated. In truth, he didn't know where to begin. Would he say he had gone for a job interview and ended up in a kidnapping gone wrong? That he had fought his way out with blood on his hands and ghosts trailing behind him? That he had been saved by a village girl who spoke like a griot and moved like a whisper? Who would believe it?

"I was kidnapped," he finally said. "In Abuja. On my way to an interview. We were about sixteen. Only I escaped."

The priest whistled softly, crossing himself. "God of mercy."

Kola leaned forward. "But the police think I'm one of them. The kidnappers. I took a gun. I killed... I didn't have a choice."

Father Mbakwe nodded slowly, as if weighing the confession against the silence of dawn. "I believe you. God sees the heart. But this country, eh? It does not always see clearly. Where are you headed now?"

"I don't know. Maybe Ogbomosho. Maybe Lagos. I just need to disappear for a while."

The priest nodded again. Then he smiled faintly. "You're in luck. I'm heading to Ibadan for a clergy retreat. I'll drop you at a safe point. But until then, you must not leave this car. There are checkpoints ahead."

....

The road was long, dotted with silent villages and shrines tucked beneath palm trees. They passed markets just waking up, women setting down baskets of peppers, children yawning beneath rusty zinc roofs. Each checkpoint brought new tension, new questions. But Father Mbakwe had a way of disarming suspicion—with his calm voice, his crisp soutane, and the large Bible always lying open on the dashboard.

At the fourth checkpoint, an officer peered into the back seat. "Who be that?"

"Ah, that's my nephew," the priest replied smoothly. "Sick boy. I'm taking him to a specialist in Ibadan. We suspect liver issues."

The officer nodded sympathetically. "Sorry oh. Make una go."

As they drove past, Kola stared at the priest with new respect.

"You're a good liar for a man of God," he said.

Father Mbakwe chuckled. "Even Jesus hid sometimes. Wisdom is not sin."

They arrived in Ibadan by late afternoon. The city buzzed with noise and life. Hawkers weaved between cars, shouting about gala and cold malt. Music blared from keke napeps. Ibadan was chaos wearing a face of familiarity.

The priest parked in front of a run-down compound off Sango Road. It had peeling paint and a sagging fence, but the spirit of safety clung to it like incense.

"This place belongs to a retired nun," the priest said. "You can stay here for two nights. After that, you must move. The police will come knocking soon."

Kola nodded. "Thank you, Father. I owe you my life."

"No, you owe God. Just make sure you don't waste the second chance He's given you."

As the priest drove off, Kola entered the house. Inside was dim, smelled of Dettol and old rosaries. The nun, a tiny woman with sharp eyes and a voice like dry okro, said nothing, just pointed to a room and handed him a plate of rice.

....

That night, sleep eluded him. He lay on the mat, listening to the creaks of the house, the distant barking of dogs, and the low murmur of his own guilt. He saw the faces of the men he'd shot. He heard the scream of the woman who died beside him in the van. He saw Halima's eyes, her mouth set in brave silence.

Around 2 AM, he heard a knock.

Three knocks. Then silence.

He rose, barefoot, crept to the window, and peered out.

Two figures. One tall. One shorter. Both in dark clothing.

Then a whisper. "Kola. Kola, na me."

His heart nearly stopped.

Halima.

He opened the door slightly. "What—how? How did you find me?"

She stepped in, eyes wild. "No time. You gats follow me now."

"What? Why?"

"One of the boys from Moro see us that night. He talk. They tell police. They dey come here now."

Kola's mouth went dry. "Jesus."

"No time to pray. Dress. I get bike outside."

The nun appeared, eyes blazing. "What is this? Who is she?"

"No worry, Mama," Halima said. "I dey save your boy from wahala."

To her shock, the nun nodded. "Go. But don't come back. God be with you."

The night air stung his eyes as the motorcycle sped through Ibadan's narrow streets. Halima drove like she was possessed. They cut through backroads, past sleeping mosques and drunk night guards. At one point, a checkpoint appeared.

Halima didn't stop.

A gunshot rang out.

They ducked, swerved, nearly hit a truck.

When they finally stopped, far beyond Bodija, under an abandoned flyover, Kola jumped off, chest heaving.

"You're insane."

She grinned. "You dey alive abi?"

He looked at her, at her eyes full of fire, at her lips curled in defiance.

"Why are you doing all this?"

Her smile faded. "Because if I don't, nobody will. My brother died in that same kidnapping van. I saw the list of victims. I know what they did to you. And I know this country no get justice unless person carry am for head like basin."

Kola sat on a block. Silent. Moved beyond words.

She sat beside him. "We go plan now. You no fit run forever. We go record video. Tell your story. Put am online. Let the world hear the truth."

He looked at her. "And if they come for us?" Her voice dropped. "Then we fight. Twice the devil they send, twice the fire we give."

Chapter Eight: Ashes and Echoes

The wind over Ibadan that morning was not the kind that merely cooled, it whispered warnings, carried the scent of burning tyre and rain-soaked dust. Kola and Halima crouched beneath the crumbling flyover, backs pressed to concrete, hands trembling with urgency. The early traffic was beginning to build, hawkers shouting prices, Danfo buses coughing black smoke into the air. But here in the shadows, time hung like a guillotine.

Halima unzipped the small black backpack she'd slung over her shoulder. Out came a second-hand smartphone with a cracked screen, a black scarf, and a small dictaphone.

Kola raised an eyebrow. "We're going to take down the Nigerian police force with a recorder and a Tecno phone?"

She didn't laugh. "We're going to tell the truth. The whole truth. If they want to bury it, they will have to bury me too."

Kola looked at her closely for the first time since the rescue. The weariness had begun to show on her face, under her eyes. But behind it, her resolve burned like stubborn coal. This was no ordinary village girl. Halima had grit in her blood.

"Talk," she said. "Everything. Start from the bus, Abuja, all the way to Moro. No lies."

He hesitated.

"People died, Halima. I killed. I ran. I stole."

"Good. Say it. Nigeria dey hear criminals confess every day. Let them hear a victim for once."

He nodded slowly. Swallowed. Then began.

"My name is Kola, full name Kolapo Samuel Adeoye. I was kidnapped on my way to an interview in Abuja. I was one of sixteen passengers in that bus. They stopped us on the Lokoja express. I thought it was SARS at first—until they killed the driver."

He told it all. His voice broke twice, once when recounting the old man who died praying, and again when describing the girl who bled out while he played dead. Halima never interrupted, only clicked the record button again whenever the phone went off.

When he finished, she handed him a sachet of pure water.

"This one go shake them."

"What next?"

"We upload it. But not now. First, we get safe."

Their safe house came courtesy of Halima's cousin, a rugged-looking youth named Kabir who lived in the burnt remains of an old tailoring shop in Oke-Ado. He wore oversized sunglasses, always had a toothpick in his mouth, and called everyone "comrade."

"You people carry wahala reach my domot, abi?" Kabir grinned, unlocking the padlock to the iron gate.

"No be wahala," Halima said. "Na truth."

Inside was dusty, with torn curtains and a fan that worked only when you slapped it three times. But it was safe. Kabir connected them to a small online community of citizen reporters and rogue journalists. One woman, who went by the alias 'MamaX,' agreed to amplify the recording once it dropped.

"You have 48 hours," MamaX said through a voice note. "After that, I won't risk it. My last story almost got me stabbed in Yaba."

"Deal," Halima replied.

They planned the release like revolutionaries. They edited the audio, added background footage of the crime scene Halima had secretly filmed on her phone, masked Kola's face with AI filters, and wrote a gripping caption:

"Confession of a Survivor: How I Escaped Death on Nigeria's Deadliest Road."

....

Two nights later, the video went live on X and Instagram.

Within one hour, it had 10,000 views.

By dawn, it had been shared by influencers, student unions, and even an angry senator's aide.

By 9 AM, two major dailies had quoted it in breaking stories.

By 11 AM, the Nigerian Police Force released a statement:

"The authorities are currently investigating claims made in a viral video. Members of the public are advised to avoid spreading unverified information."

Kola sat frozen in Kabir's shop, eyes locked on the screen. "It's happening," he whispered. "They know now."

Halima didn't smile. "Wait till nightfall. That's when demons really wake."

She was right.

At 8:13 PM, Kabir's phone rang. He checked the screen, then frowned.

"Unknown number. Long digits."

"Don't pick," Halima said.

It rang again.

Then again.

Then it stopped.

Three minutes later, the shop's light flickered. Then darkness.

Kabir moved fast. "Generator wire don cut. Or maybe no be gen."

Outside, footsteps. Not one. Not two. Many.

Halima grabbed her duffel.

"Kola, now!"

They burst out the back, through the tailor's old workshop. Over stacks of broken chairs, across a fence. The night air swallowed them.

They ran like hunted animals, Kabir taking a different route to divert attention. Kola's legs burned. His ribs screamed. But fear has a way of extending strength.

By midnight, they found refuge in Dugbe, in a church's unfinished compound. The caretaker was asleep. Halima had to bribe him with N500 and a cigarette.

They collapsed behind a stack of concrete blocks. Halima's hands were bleeding. Kola's ankle throbbed.

"This is madness," Kola muttered. "We're going to die."

"No," Halima whispered. "We're going to win."

But death had not given up the chase.

The following morning, MamaX sent them a voice note. Her hideout had been raided. Phones smashed. Laptops seized. She barely escaped.

"They want your heads, Kola. The people you exposed, this thing reach high places."

Halima nodded. "It always does."

They decided it was time to leave Ibadan.

Halima called her uncle in Ilorin, a retired immigration officer with enough grey hair to scare police. He agreed to hide them for a week.

"You two better not bring bullet to my compound," he warned. "I like my peace."

They boarded a night bus, dressed as a married couple, Halima in a gele and fake bump, Kola in borrowed agbada and dark glasses.

Ilorin greeted them with early harmattan winds and a quiet that felt too clean to trust. The uncle lived in a quiet street in Tanke, with two cats and a wife who didn't ask questions.

Kola rested for the first time in days. Ate semo. Drank malt. Listened to Halima snore. He even smiled.

But trouble was not done. Two days later, a call came. This time, from Lagos. A human rights lawyer had seen the video.

"I believe your story," the man said. "And I want to help you. We can file a case. Sue the authorities. Demand an investigation."

Kola stared at Halima.

"A court case? With my face?"

Halima nodded. "Maybe it's time."

The lawyer arranged to meet them at the University of Ilorin campus. A public place. Neutral.

They arrived early. Sat on the stone benches by the fountain. Students passed them, oblivious.

Then a voice.

"Kola?"

He turned. A man in suit. Clean. Polite smile. No tie.

But his eyes were cold.

Then two more men appeared behind him.

Not students. Not lawyers.

Guns under their jackets.

Halima whispered, "Run."

Kola didn't move, couldn't.

The suited man stepped closer. "You should have stayed dead."

Chapter Nine: Echoes in the Dark

Ibadan, even as night curled around the city like an old mosquito net, it buzzed faintly—bikes murmuring down alleys, night preachers casting out unseen demons, and the distant clink of bottles from local joints. But in the safe house beneath the rusting flyover where Kola and Halima had taken shelter, it was the silence between those sounds that felt loudest.

Halima sat by the doorway, eyes scanning the street as if expecting a ghost. Kola paced inside, too restless to sleep, too tired to think straight. The glow from a small rechargeable lantern cast strange shadows on the peeling walls.

"We can't stay here much longer," Halima said finally.

"I know," Kola replied. "But where next? We've run out of miracles."

She stood, pulling a crumpled paper from her satchel. It was a contact card. Faded, water-stained, but the name was still legible: Dapo Fakoya — Investigative Journalist, The Morning Torch.

"I met him once at a youth event in Zaria," Halima said. "He told me, 'If you ever come across something Nigeria must hear, call me.' I think this is it."

Kola stared at the card like it was a holy relic. "You think he'll believe us?"

"We don't need belief. We need someone reckless enough to publish the truth."

Kola took the phone Halima handed him and dialed.

They met Dapo two days later in a dusty, inconspicuous corner of Dugbe. He wore glasses that didn't fit properly and had the look of someone who hadn't slept in weeks. But his eyes were sharp, and his voice steady.

"Before you say anything," he said, "know that if you're lying, I'll bury the story and call the police."

Kola nodded. "Fair."

For the next two hours, they talked. Kola laid out everything—the bus ride, the hijack, the slaughter, the escape, the police hunt. Halima filled in details from Moro, her own escape, and how they'd been moving like shadows since.

Dapo listened without a word. When they finished, he simply leaned back and closed his eyes.

"You've stepped into a hornet's nest," he said. "These men... they have people in the police, in politics. But if we play this right, we can burn it all."

He reached into his bag and pulled out a voice recorder.

"We'll start with a proper interview. I'll verify what I can. Then we film you—masked if you prefer. Once the story's out, they'll either kill us, or run scared. Depends who listens first."

Kola swallowed hard. "Let's do it."

By the weekend, Dapo had pieced together a damning audio-visual story. He traced the corrupt police commissioner whose men had leaked Kola's photo. He dug into the land in Moro where the massacre happened—linked it to an oil syndicate trying to displace the villagers. And he obtained blurry footage from a petrol station showing Kola fleeing with a bloodied AK47.

When the story went live under the title "Twice the Devil: The Blood on Nigeria's Quiet Roads", it spread like wildfire.

Twitter. Facebook. Blogs. Radio stations.

It was all anyone could talk about for three days straight.

"Anonymous survivor exposes state-police complicity in brutal Abuja kidnapping."

"Who is the mystery tech graduate behind Nigeria's newest whistleblower story?"

Then came the backlash.

Halima was nearly caught in Mokola by plainclothes officers. Kola's image appeared on a 'Wanted' flyer outside UI gate. Dapo's office was broken into. A flash drive stolen. His editor received a brown envelope and a simple message: "Kill the story or it kills you."

They had to move again.

This time to Abeokuta, where Dapo had an aunt who ran a decrepit boarding house for JAMB students. The old woman, half-blind and loud as a bell, didn't ask questions. She called Kola "Brother Laptop" and gave Halima kitchen duty.

In the nights, they strategized.

"We can't hide forever," Halima said. "We need allies."

"Public figures," Dapo added. "Human rights lawyers. Churches. Even foreign embassies. If they know you, they can't erase you."

That was how Kola ended up on a Twitter Spaces with a popular activist pastor who simply went by "P. Moses." Halfway through the session, the cleric shouted:

"Every time our youth rise, demons in agbada try to silence them. But God has not given us a spirit of fear! My church is backing this boy!"

The next morning, Kola's face trended across Africa.

That same day, two men were found dead in a compound in Ogbomosho.

Dapo read the news aloud: "Ex-police officers linked to kidnapping ring found murdered. No suspects yet."

Kola's hands shook as he read the names.

They were two of the men from that van. The ones who had laughed as they shot the woman beside him.

"Someone's cleaning house," he murmured.

They knew the heat would return.

It did, tenfold.

An unmarked car began circling the Abeokuta house. A cousin of Dapo was arrested on vague charges. The retired nun in Ibadan was beaten. Halima received a note: *"Even stones break."*

"We need to move again," Dapo said.

But Halima shook her head. "No. We fight now." She opened a folder.

Inside were bank statements, location logs, and a list of names. "I hacked one of the kidnappers' phones before it got wiped. There's enough here to destroy more than a ring—ministers, officers, even a senator."

Kola stared at the files. "How did you...?"

Halima smiled. "You think na only you sabi tech? I've been coding since secondary school."

They leaked the documents in stages. One day, it was a video of a commissioner accepting bribes. Next, call logs between a Lagos businessman and an arms dealer.

Then came the voice message: a senator demanding a 'cleanup' in Moro.

The fallout was seismic.

Protests erupted. Students marched. Newspapers screamed headlines.

Then, just as the wave of outrage reached its peak—Dapo disappeared.

No warning. No phone call. Nothing.

His aunt found his phone in a gutter near Kuto market. Blood on the case.

Kola didn't cry. He sat for hours staring at a wall, lips moving silently.

"We keep going," Halima said, voice breaking.

Kola nodded.

"Twice the devil they send," he said, "twice the fire we give."

But fire consumes. One night, as they prepared to flee again, a message pinged on Kola's phone.

It was a number he didn't recognize.

We know where you are. You have 12 hours. Silence is survival.

He looked at Halima. "We need a last move. A big one."

She nodded. "We crash their servers."

"What?"

"Every trace of their network—their finances, their communication, their shell companies—it's all digital. You and I can wipe it. But we do it loud. So loud that if we vanish, the echo stays."

They worked all night.

Kola wrote code like a man possessed. Halima patched through stolen VPNs. They breached a private security firm's firewall. Flooded the mainframe. Planted a deadman's switch: if they didn't log in every 24 hours, all data would be published.

At 5:03 a.m., it was done.

Kola looked at her. "No going back now." She kissed him on the forehead. "We never were."

Chapter Ten: A Fire Untamed

Dawn arrived on Abeokuta with the hush of withheld breath. It was the kind of morning that carried no birdsong, only the quiet hum of tension. Kola and Halima had barely slept. Their eyes were puffy, their limbs taut. The air in the room tasted like electricity and fear.

Outside, the streets were waking up—the shouts of hawkers, clatter of wheelbarrows, honks of danfo buses. But inside the old boarding house, it felt like time had stalled.

"Is it done?" Halima asked.

Kola nodded slowly. "The deadman's switch is live. If we don't check in every 24 hours, the entire archive spills onto the web."

She exhaled, almost laughing. "We just threw a match into a room full of petrol."

Before Kola could respond, the old landlady banged on their door. "You get visitor!" she barked. "Say him name na Pastor Moses!"

They froze.

....

P. Moses sat in the parlour like a man on a mission. He wore a cream agbada with 'REVIVAL' stitched across the chest and a face flushed with urgency.

"I had to come," he said, standing to greet them. "Your story has crossed oceans. CNN, BBC, Al Jazeera, they're all reaching out. But more importantly, the youth—they've risen."

Halima squinted at him. "What do you want?"

He raised both hands. "To help. You need sanctuary. I have a church compound in Enugu. Heavily guarded. We can move you there and arrange a press conference with international media."

Kola looked unsure. "You're not afraid they'll come for you too?"

The pastor smiled. "Let them come. When lions gather, the jackals scatter."

They left Abeokuta at dusk in an unmarked Toyota Sienna, driven by one of the pastor's assistants. The journey was long, winding through Osogbo, then Nsukka before arriving at the outskirts of Enugu. The compound looked modest from outside but was a fortress within—CCTV cameras, plainclothes guards, thick iron gates.

Inside, they found a room waiting, equipped with laptops, cameras, and a secure Wi-Fi hub.

But peace was not long-lasting.

That night, while Halima uploaded more files to an encrypted backup, Kola stepped out for air. He wandered the compound's garden path, only to hear hurried whispers beyond the fence.

"...he fit dey here. I saw them enter...they're hiding them..."

He ducked, heart hammering.

He ran back in. "They've found us."

Pastor Moses immediately summoned his guards. "We must evacuate. Now."

They fled under the cover of darkness again, this time toward a safehouse in Obudu provided by a local NGO. But halfway through Cross River, their convoy was ambushed.

It happened in seconds. A tire burst. Then gunshots. The driver swerved. Screams.

Kola pulled Halima down as bullets riddled the windows.

Two guards fired back from the rear vehicle. One took a shot to the neck and dropped.

"Run!" shouted Moses, blood on his agbada.

Kola and Halima burst through the thickets by the roadside, crawling through red earth, heartbeats like war drums.

Behind them, the gunfire became distant. Then a scream. Then silence.

They didn't stop until they reached a stream.

They collapsed.

Halima turned to him. "We've become fugitives of truth."

Kola's voice was hollow. "What if we lose?"

She gripped his hand. "Then let history know we tried."

In Obudu, the NGO workers treated their wounds and offered a temporary shelter. But now the stakes had changed. Someone was not just trying to silence them—they were eliminating witnesses.

Two days later, they received a message from Dapo's burner account.

I'm alive. Hidden. Trust no one. The senator has hired mercenaries. They're not police. They don't ask questions.

Kola stared at the screen, his pulse quickening.

"He's alive."

Halima blinked in disbelief. "How?"

"Doesn't matter. He's reaching out. That means he has more."

Their final move was set in motion.

They contacted a South African documentary crew interested in their story. The crew agreed to fly them to Johannesburg if they could reach Calabar.

But the road to Calabar was treacherous. Every bus station was crawling with plainclothes men. Kola shaved his head. Halima dressed as a market woman.

They slipped into an old Peugeot 504 shared taxi and prayed.

At a military checkpoint near Itu, a soldier eyed Kola suspiciously.

"Where you dey go?"

"Calabar. To bury my uncle," Kola lied.

The soldier stared, then waved them on.

As they pulled away, Halima exhaled sharply. "That was close."

In Calabar, the crew met them at a guesthouse. Cameras rolled. Lights burned. They told it all again, every betrayal, every coded file, every whisper of resistance.

Before boarding the flight, Kola turned to Halima. "If this is the last thing we ever do…"

She interrupted him with a kiss. "Then let it be worth it."

They boarded the plane as unknowns. But as the wheels lifted off the runway, their story had already begun to roar across continents.

The fire they started was no longer theirs.

It belonged to the world now.

CHAPTER 11: THE ROAD EATS ITS CHILDREN

The sun had barely woken when Kola's battered Peugeot 406 rolled onto the expressway, its engine coughing like an old man reluctant to rise. The road stretched ahead, grey and endless, cutting through the belly of the land like a scar. This was the Lagos–Kaduna expressway, the kind of road that swallowed men whole. In the silence of the car, you could almost hear it breathing—an old, patient predator that had learned to wait.

Kola sat at the wheel, his shoulders hunched forward, his eyes locked on the patch of road illuminated by the weak morning light. Beside him, Halima clutched a nylon bag against her chest, the kind of bag women carried when all they had left could fit into one space. The smell of dried fish and old perfume drifted from it. In the back seat, Baba Layi, their contact, sat with his walking stick laid across his knees. His white kaftan was rumpled, his eyes half-closed, not from sleep, but from that wary watchfulness old men carried after years of living with trouble.

The journey had no music. Even the radio had gone quiet after a few crackles of static. The air was thick with the unspoken, the danger waiting on the road, the ghosts following close behind.

"By the time we reach Jere," Baba Layi finally said, his voice a low rumble, "we'll face the worst of them. The soldiers, the police, the boys with their own guns... all of them hungry."

Halima shifted uncomfortably. "Hungry?"

He gave a humourless chuckle. "Hungry for money. Hungry for power. Hungry for blood. Out here, child, everyone eats something."

Kola kept his eyes on the road, but the muscle in his jaw twitched. "We'll give them something small and pass."

"That's what everyone thinks," Baba Layi replied, "until the road decides otherwise."

They passed through the first checkpoint easily enough, a couple of policemen leaning against a rusted Hilux, their rifles slung carelessly. One waved them through after Kola pressed a folded N500 note into his hand. But each checkpoint after that tightened the air in the car a little more. The men they met wore sterner faces, their rifles gripped tighter.

At one, a soldier leaned into the car, his eyes scanning their faces with an expression that seemed to scrape the skin off their thoughts. He sniffed once, as though he could smell fear. "Where una dey go?"

"Kaduna," Kola replied evenly.

The soldier's gaze shifted to Halima, then to the bag on her lap. "Open am."

Halima's hands trembled as she untied the knot. Inside was nothing but two wrappers, a tin of powdered milk, and a small framed photo of her mother. The soldier stared at it for a long second, then stepped back and waved them on.

The sun climbed higher. The road grew lonelier. The villages they passed became smaller and poorer, their huts crouching low as though afraid to be seen. Sometimes they saw other vehicles, tankers groaning under the weight of fuel, buses crammed with people like human cargo—but more often it was just them, the tarmac, and the long shadow of the Peugeot stretching ahead.

It was almost noon when they reached the checkpoint outside Rijana. There were more men here, dressed in mismatched uniforms, some with police insignia, some without any at all. A single barrel blocked the road, and beside it, an old wooden table littered with sachet water and empty cigarette packs.

One of the men stepped forward, tall and broad-shouldered, his beret pulled low. His eyes narrowed the moment they landed on Kola.

"You," he said. "Step down."

Kola felt the bottom drop out of his stomach. He knew that voice.

Halima's head snapped toward him. "Kola?" she whispered.

But he didn't answer. His legs felt heavy as he pushed the door open and stepped into the heat. The man with the beret came closer, a slow, deliberate smile spreading across his face.

"I know you," the man said. "You think you fit just waka pass like say nothing happen?"

"I think you're mistaken," Kola replied, his voice steady, though his palms were slick with sweat.

The man laughed, but it wasn't friendly. "Mistaken? You forget my face? Abuja, 2017. That day we raid the warehouse. You dey there, no?"

Kola's mind was already racing. Abuja, 2017… yes. The man was Sergeant Abubakar. Back then, Kola had been running a job for someone in the black market. It had ended in bullets and blood. Abubakar had taken a bullet in the shoulder. And now here he was, standing between Kola and the rest of the road.

Baba Layi leaned out of the window. "Oga officer, we fit settle this matter like men," he said, pulling a folded wad of notes from his breast pocket. "Make the road no hear bad story."

But Abubakar's eyes never left Kola's face. "This one no be about money," he said slowly. "This one na about memory."

He took a step forward, his hand drifting toward the rifle slung over his chest. Another man from the checkpoint moved closer. The heat thickened, heavy with the smell of dust and sweat.

Kola knew what was coming before it happened. His hand went to the pistol hidden under his shirt.

"Don't," Halima's voice cracked behind him.

Too late.

The moment Abubakar's fingers brushed the rifle, the first shot rang out. It was unclear who fired first, but in an instant, the air erupted into chaos—shouts, gunfire, the clanging sound of bullets hitting metal. Baba Layi dropped low inside the car, yelling for Halima to do the same. The smell of gunpowder bit into their throats.

Kola ducked behind the open car door, firing twice toward the men by the barrel. One fell. Another scrambled for cover. But the road was wide open, and the Peugeot had nowhere to hide.

A scream tore through the air. It wasn't Halima.

When Kola turned, his stomach clenched. A young boy—no more than ten—lay sprawled in the dust by the side of the road. He must have been selling boiled groundnuts to travelers before the shooting began. His basket was overturned, the nuts scattered into the sand like marbles.

Kola's heart slammed against his ribs.

Abubakar shouted something, but the words were lost in the gunfire. Then, just as suddenly as it started, the shooting stopped. A silence fell, broken only by the ragged breathing of the men still standing.

Everyone's eyes were on the boy.

Halima was the first to move. She ran to the child, kneeling beside him, her hands trembling as she pressed against the wound in his chest. Blood seeped through her fingers.

"He's still breathing!" she cried. "Kola, help me!"

Kola hesitated, the pistol still heavy in his hand. His gaze flicked to Abubakar, who was standing very still now, his rifle lowered, his face unreadable.

Finally, Kola shoved the gun into his waistband and ran forward. Between the three of them: Kola, Halima, and Baba Layi—they lifted the boy and laid him gently in the back seat.

Abubakar stepped aside without a word as Kola started the car again. But as they pulled away, Kola caught his eyes in the rearview mirror. It was a look that promised their paths would cross again.

The Peugeot sped down the road, the boy's faint breathing a fragile thread in the back seat. Halima kept whispering to him, as if her voice alone could keep him tethered to life.

Baba Layi's face was grim. "The road has taken its tithe," he said quietly.

Kola didn't answer. His hands gripped the wheel until his knuckles went white. He had known the road would be dangerous. But he hadn't expected it to remember his sins—and throw them back at him with such precision.

And somewhere deep inside, he knew this was only the beginning.

Chapter 12: Harvest of the Dead

The road into the village was not a road at all but a memory of one — a scar in the earth, pitted with ruts that filled with water whenever the rains came. Now, in the dry harmattan light, the ruts were hard as bone, each jolt of the pickup truck throwing dust into their throats. The driver said nothing. Neither did Kola or Halima. They were all listening, in their own way, to the sound of the place.

Villages had their own sounds. This one whispered in the wind like someone telling a secret from far away — the slow creak of palm fronds, the dry scrape of goats rubbing themselves against fence posts, the thin echo of a child's laughter that seemed too fragile to survive the season.

Kola had thought the city was loud with corruption, but here, silence was the heavier thing.

They stopped before a building that pretended to be a court but was more of a shrine with ambitions. The roof sagged under the weight of rust. Two columns of cracked cement held up the entrance, their surfaces scored with graffiti — some in chalk, some in knife scratches. A crucifix hung beside a small carving of *Eshu*, the trickster.

"Here," the driver said, as if speaking more would invite trouble.

Inside, it was cooler, but not by much. The ceiling fan turned like a drunk who could not decide whether to collapse. Benches had been arranged in rows, their wood darkened by years of sweat and arguments. The people of the village had come — old men with walking sticks, women with headscarves pulled tight, children crouching low to see without being told to go away. At the far end, on a raised platform, the judge sat.

He was an old Yoruba man, his beard trimmed close, his face neither kind nor cruel but carved with the patience of someone who had seen storms break and return again. On his left wrist, Catholic rosary beads clicked softly when he moved. On his right, faint scars marked the signs of Ifá initiation. He carried both faiths the way some men carried both debts and promises.

"Bring the man forward," the judge said. His voice was not loud, but the room obeyed.

Kola stepped into the open space, the dust making halos in the light that fell through the broken slats of the window.

The charges were read. They sounded different here — stripped of the pomp of city courts, reduced to their bones. *Suspicion of violence. Interference with the king's peace. Bringing death upon another.*

The words hung like smoke. Kola wanted to say that the world had already accused him of worse, but here, in this place, it felt like every word carried its own weight in iron.

The judge leaned forward. "You came from the road."

"Yes."

"The road eats its children," the judge said. "Do you know this?"

Kola hesitated. "I have heard."

"Then you know the road does not spit them back the same."

The trial, if it could be called that, began. But it was not about witnesses or evidence. Instead, the judge called for stories. One by one, villagers spoke — not of Kola directly, but of the road, the army, the bribes, the losses that had been paid not in money but in sons and daughters.

A woman told of her brother who had gone to Lagos to drive a taxi and was found on the side of the highway, his pockets turned inside out. An old man spoke of a bribe he refused to pay, and how his yam harvest was mysteriously ruined three days later. A boy, no older than twelve, stood and said simply: "The road took my father. I don't go near it anymore."

Through it all, the judge listened. The rosary beads clicked. The Ifá scars caught the light.

When it was Kola's turn, the room seemed to lean in.

He did not speak of every sin. He could not. But he told them about the checkpoint, about the officer who recognized him, about the bribe that turned into gunfire, about the man who had died without knowing why. His voice cracked only once, when he spoke of the dust that settled on the man's eyes before anyone thought to close them.

When he finished, the judge was silent for a long time. Then he spoke.

"There is a saying," the judge began. "The man who kills the devil twice will wear his face in the dark."

The villagers murmured. Halima, sitting in the back, tilted her head.

"This means," the judge continued, "that when you fight evil the same way twice, you become like the thing you fight. You may tell yourself you are only surviving, but the darkness does not care for your reasons. It only cares for your face."

There was no verdict. Only that parable. The judge stood, and the court dissolved into talk. People filed out, their sandals scraping the floor.

Kola stood in the emptying space, not sure whether he had been freed or sentenced to something more invisible.

Outside, the harmattan light was sharp, almost metallic. Halima came to him. "What now?" she asked.

He looked past her, at the road curling out of the village like a snake unsure if it should strike. "We leave," he said.

They found a ride to Cotonou — a battered Peugeot with one working door. The journey was slow. At every stop, Kola felt the eyes of strangers lingering too long, as if they could read the parable on his skin.

By the time they reached the city, the day had folded into night. They walked until they found a café — small, with yellow walls that had seen better years. A ceiling fan spun above, moving the air but not cooling it.

Kola ordered tea he didn't drink. He took out a notebook, the cheap kind with the corners already curling, and began to write.

The first line came without thinking:

I make bad decisions until it becomes a tree ripe for harvest.

He wrote about the road, about the faces of the dead, about the judge whose wrist carried two faiths. He wrote as if writing could pin the shadows down. Halima sat across from him, sipping slowly, watching the street outside where motorbikes coughed past.

Somewhere, a siren wailed, then faded.

Kola kept writing, knowing the harvest was still coming.

Glossary

Àbíkú (Yoruba) – A spirit child believed to die and be reborn repeatedly, often seen as a harbinger of tragedy.

Adura (Yoruba) – Prayer, often offered in the form of chants or spoken petitions to God or the *Orishas*.

Agbada (Yoruba) – Flowing wide-sleeved robe worn by men, symbol of status and dignity.

Àṣẹ (Yoruba) – The spiritual command or life force that makes things happen, often invoked in blessings.

Babaláwo (Yoruba) – A high priest in Ifá divination, keeper of secrets and wisdom.

Cotonou – The bustling economic hub of Benin Republic, a city of contradictions: sea breezes and diesel fumes.

Egúngún (Yoruba) – Masquerades representing ancestral spirits, draped in layers of cloth and mystery.

Ifá (Yoruba) – A complex system of divination and philosophy practiced by Yoruba people.

Juju – West African spiritual practice involving charms, spells, and ritual power.

Kokoro (Yoruba) – Literally "insect," but often used metaphorically to mean a hidden danger or secret weakness.

Oba (Yoruba) – King or traditional ruler.

Ọ̀pá Ọ̀runmìlà (Yoruba) – The diviner's staff, sacred to the god of wisdom, *Ọ̀runmìlà*.

Ogun (Yoruba) – The *god* of iron, war, and labor, feared for his temper and strength.

Ọjà (Yoruba) – Market; a place of trade, gossip, and the hum of everyday survival.

Ọmọlúàbí (Yoruba) – A person of good character, raised with respect, truth, and honor.

Ṣàngó (Yoruba) – The god of thunder, lightning, and fire—patron of justice and quick wrath.